Dear Parents and Educators,

Welcome to Penguin Young Readers! As parents and educators, you know that each child develops at his or her own pace—in terms of speech, critical thinking, and, of course, reading. Penguin Young Readers recognizes this fact. As a result, each Penguin Young Readers book is assigned a traditional easy-to-read level (1–4) as well as a Guided Reading Level (A–P). Both of these systems will help you choose the right book for your child. Please refer to the back of each book for specific leveling information. Penguin Young Readers features esteemed authors and illustrators, stories about favorite characters, fascinating nonfiction, and more!

The Tale of Benjamin Bunny

LEVEL **2**

GUIDED READING LEVEL **I**

This book is perfect for a **Progressing Reader** who:
• can figure out unknown words by using picture and context clues;
• can recognize beginning, middle, and ending sounds;
• can make and confirm predictions about what will happen in the text; and
• can distinguish between fiction and nonfiction.

Here are some **activities** you can do during and after reading this book:
• Sight Words: Sight words are frequently used words that readers must know just by looking at them. These words are known instantly, on sight. Knowing these words helps children develop into efficient readers. The sight words listed below appear in this book. As you read the story, have the child point out the sight words.

his	out	saw	their	those	very	were
one	put	some	they	two	was	your

• Compare/Contrast: Benjamin Bunny and Peter Rabbit are cousins. Discuss the ways in which they are alike and different.

Remember, sharing the love of reading with a child is the best gift you can give!

—Bonnie Bader, EdM
   Penguin Young Readers program

*Penguin Young Readers are leveled by independent reviewers applying the standards developed by Irene Fountas and Gay Su Pinnell in *Matching Books to Readers: Using Leveled Books in Guided Reading*, Heinemann, 1999.

Penguin Young Readers
Published by the Penguin Group
Penguin Group (USA) Inc., 375 Hudson Street, New York, New York 10014, USA
Penguin Group (Canada), 90 Eglinton Avenue East, Suite 700, Toronto, Ontario M4P 2Y3, Canada
(a division of Pearson Penguin Canada Inc.)
Penguin Books Ltd., 80 Strand, London WC2R 0RL, England
Penguin Group Ireland, 25 St. Stephen's Green, Dublin 2, Ireland (a division of Penguin Books Ltd.)
Penguin Group (Australia), 250 Camberwell Road, Camberwell, Victoria 3124, Australia
(a division of Pearson Australia Group Pty. Ltd.)
Penguin Books India Pvt. Ltd., 11 Community Centre, Panchsheel Park, New Delhi—110 017, India
Penguin Group (NZ), 67 Apollo Drive, Rosedale, Auckland 0632, New Zealand
(a division of Pearson New Zealand Ltd.)
Penguin Books (South Africa) (Pty.) Ltd., 24 Sturdee Avenue,
Rosebank, Johannesburg 2196, South Africa

Penguin Books Ltd., Registered Offices: 80 Strand, London WC2R 0RL, England

Visit our website at: www.peterrabbit.com

Color reproduction by Saxon Photolitho.

Library of Congress Cataloging-in-Publication Data is available.

ISBN 978-0-7232-6814-7   10 9 8 7 6 5 4

The Tale of Benjamin Bunny

TM

based on the original tale by Beatrix Potter

Penguin Young Readers
An Imprint of Penguin Group (USA) Inc.

This is the tale of

Benjamin Bunny.

One morning he sat

in the woods.

Benjamin Bunny saw a cart on
the road.

Mr. and Mrs. McGregor were in
the cart.

They were going out for the day.

Benjamin ran to tell his cousin
Peter Rabbit.

Benjamin looked behind a tree.

He saw two little ears

sticking out.

It was his cousin Peter Rabbit.

Peter was wrapped in a small,

red cloth.

Benjamin sat next to Peter.

"Peter, who has your clothes?"

Peter told Benjamin that he had

been chased by Mr. McGregor.

Peter had dropped his coat and

shoes in Mr. McGregor's garden.

Now Mr. McGregor was using

Peter's clothes for a scarecrow!

"Come along, Peter," said Benjamin.

"Mr. and Mrs. McGregor have gone out in their cart.

Let's go and find your clothes."

Benjamin and Peter stood on the garden wall.

They could see Peter's shoes and coat on the scarecrow.

There was a big, green hat on the scarecrow, too.

Benjamin and Peter climbed

down a pear tree into the

garden.

Peter fell, but he was not hurt.

Peter put on his blue coat.

Benjamin put on the green hat.

It was much too big for him!

Then Benjamin and Peter
collected onions for
Peter's mother.
They put them in the small,
red cloth.

As they walked through the garden, Benjamin munched on a lettuce leaf.

But Peter Rabbit felt very scared

in Mr. McGregor's garden.

He was so scared that he

dropped half of the onions.

Some brown mice watched as Benjamin and Peter tried to find their way out of the garden.

Suddenly, the little rabbits

stopped walking.

They saw something.

It was a cat!

They hid under a basket.

The cat walked over to the

basket.

She sat down on top of it!

The cat sat there for a very

long time.

Benjamin and Peter were

very scared.

On the wall above the cat,

Benjamin's father,

old Mr. Bunny,

was walking along.

He was looking for his son.

Old Mr. Bunny jumped down

from the wall and pushed the cat

off the basket.

Then he took the small, red cloth of onions and marched those two naughty rabbits home.

That night, the onions were hung
in the kitchen.

Peter and his sister Cotton-tail
folded up the small, red cloth.